I CAN READ BY MYSELF

ILLUSTRATED BY ERIC KINCAID AND PAMELA STOREY
WRITTEN BY LUCY KINCAID

BRIMAX BOOKS · NEWMARKET · ENGLAND

Here is a collection of amusing animal
stories with a very simple repetitive
text primarily designed for children of
4-7 years who are ready to read. The
text is presented in large type. In
addition to each story is a special
section to encourage the revision of
new words and concepts to stimulate
observation and memory.
Children will love the easy-to-follow
adventures of Polly Pig, Hedgehog,
Little Hamster, Cheepy Chick, Dragon
and their animal friends.

ISBN 0 86112 295 X
© BRIMAX RIGHTS LTD 1985. All rights reserved.
These stories also appear as individual books.
Published by BRIMAX BOOKS 1985.
Printed in Belgium

Contents

DRAGON and SLEEPY OWL

Dragon lives in the wood.
He has many friends.
Owl is Dragon's friend.
Owl is on his way home.

Owl has been out all night.
He has been very busy.
Owl is very tired. He goes
to sleep. Along comes Fox.
"Wake up, Owl," says Fox.
"I want to talk to you."
Owl wakes up.
He listens to Fox.

Fox has gone. Owl is asleep. Along comes Rabbit.
"Wake up, Owl," says Rabbit. "I want to talk to you."
Owl wakes up.
He listens to Rabbit.

All the animals want to talk to Owl. Owl is very tired. He cannot work day and night.
He must get some sleep.
Owl goes to see Dragon.

"Will you stand under my tree?" says Owl. "Will you see that no one comes to talk to me? I must get some sleep."
"I will come now," says Dragon.
Owl goes back to his tree. Dragon stands under the tree.

A mouse comes to see
Owl.
Dragon growls.
The mouse runs away.
A squirrel comes to see
Owl.
Dragon growls.
The squirrel runs away.
Dragon growls when
anyone comes near the
tree.

"Are you asleep, Owl?"
says Dragon.
"No," says Owl.
"Why not?" says Dragon.
"Your growls keep me
awake," says Owl.
"I am sorry," says Dragon.
"What can I do?" says
Dragon.

The bees know what to do.
They know a sleeping
song.

"Hum Hum Hum," hum
the bees. "Close your eyes.
Go to sleep.

Hum Hum Hum."
Dragon hums too.

"Hum Hum Hum," hums
Dragon. "Close your eyes.
Go to sleep.

Hum Hum Hum."

Owl's eyes are shut.
Owl is asleep.
"Do not stop humming,"
say the birds. "Owl will
wake up if you do."
Dragon keeps on humming.
So do the bees.

HM-MM-MM-MM-MM-MM

HM-MM-MM-MM-MM-MM-MM
MM-MM-MM-MM-MM-MM

The animals listen to the song. They get sleepy. The birds listen to the song.
They get sleepy.
Soon they are all asleep.

HM-MM-MM

HM-MM-MM

HM-MM-MM

The bees are awake.
The bees are still
humming.
Dragon is still awake.
Dragon is still humming.
The bees are getting
sleepy. Dragon puts his
paws over his ears.

HM-MM-M

HM-MM-MM-MM-MM

HM-MMMMM-M-M
M-MM-M
MM-M
M-M-M

31

The bees are asleep.
Dragon is still awake.
His paws are over his ears.
Dragon cannot hear the
sleeping song.

"HM-MM-MM-MM-MM-MM"

Owl wakes up.
"I cannot hear anyone,"
says Owl.
Dragon tells him they are
all asleep.
Owl laughs when he sees
them asleep. Owl laughs
so much that they all wake
up.
And then they all laugh
too.

Say these words again

busy

friends

listen

eyes

talk

tired

squirrel

work

night

sleepy

sorry

paws

laugh

growls

What are they doing?

sleeping

standing

laughing

growling

running

37

CHEEPY CHICK'S HOLIDAY

Cheepy Chick has a shop.
The shop is full of jars. The
jars are full of sweets.
There are yellow ones,
brown ones, white ones,
pink ones and green ones.
Cheepy Chick sells a lot of
sweets. Cheepy Chick is
always busy.

Rob Rabbit wants brown
sweets. They are on the
top shelf.
Cheepy Chick gets the
ladder. Up she goes. She
gets the jar. She brings it
down.
Cheepy Chick puts some
brown sweets in a bag.
Rob Rabbit pays for the
sweets.
"Thank you," says Rob
Rabbit.

Cheepy Chick puts the jar
back on the shelf. She
comes down the ladder.
Molly Mouse comes into
the shop. Molly Mouse
wants to buy pink sweets.
They are on the middle
shelf.
Cheepy Chick moves the
ladder along.

Cheepy Chick goes up the ladder. She gets the jar from the shelf.
"I do not want pink sweets now," says Molly Mouse.
"I want white ones."
The white sweets are on the next shelf. Cheepy Chick comes down the ladder. She moves the ladder along. She goes up the ladder.

Polly Pig comes to the shop. Little Hamster and Bob Hedgehog come with her. Cheepy Chick is asleep.

"Wake up," says Polly Pig.

"Are you ill?" says Little Hamster.

"I have been very busy," says Cheepy Chick. "I am so tired."

"You need a holiday," says Polly Pig.

"Who will look after the
shop?" says Cheepy Chick.
"I will look after the shop,"
says Polly Pig.
"I will help Polly," says
Little Hamster.
"So will I," says Bob
Hedgehog.
"Go and get ready," says
Polly Pig.
Cheepy Chick gets ready to
go. Cheepy Chick is happy.

51

Cheepy Chick has lots of fun. She likes the snow. The snow is cold. Cheepy Chick is not cold.

Her hat keeps her warm. Her scarf keeps her warm. Her coat keeps her warm. Cheepy Chick falls over. The snow is soft. She is not hurt. It is fun.

Pat Penguin helps Cheepy Chick. He shows her what to do. Cheepy Chick goes very fast. She can stop when she wants to. She does not fall over.

"I like going fast," says Cheepy Chick.

"I like being on holiday," says Cheepy Chick.

Cheepy Chick is home again. Polly Pig is glad to see her. Little Hamster is glad to see her. Bob Hedgehog is glad to see her.

"We have been so busy," they say.

"We feel tired now," they say.

Cheepy Chick does not feel tired. She does not need the ladder. She hops up to the jars of sweets.
"My holiday did me good," says Cheepy Chick.
"We can see that," says Polly Pig.
They are all happy.

Say these words again

sweets	snow
full	cold
goodbye	busy
middle	thank you
holiday	tired
waves	happy
window	ready

DRAGON in THE WOOD

What can you see?

shelf

ladder

train

penguin

scarf

It is a hot day.
The birds are asleep.
The bees are asleep.
The rabbits are asleep.
All the animals are asleep.
Only the flowers are
awake.

71

The birds wake up.
The bees wake up.
The rabbits wake up.
All the animals wake up.
"What is that?" they say.

"Who is coming?" say the birds
"Who is coming?" say the animals.
"It is a dragon," say the bees.
The animals are afraid.
They all hide.
The flowers do not hide.

They all look at the dragon.
The dragon is hot.
He sits down.
They can all see the dragon.
The dragon cannot see them.
They are hiding.

What will the dragon do?
The dragon shuts his eyes.
The dragon opens his
mouth.
The dragon begins to sing.
They do not like the
dragon's song.
They all want him to stop
singing.

They all come out of
hiding.
"Stop!" say the birds.
"Stop!" say the bees.
"Stop!" say all the
animals.
The dragon stops singing.

The dragon opens his eyes.
"Where have you come
from?" says the dragon.
"We live here," say the
birds.
"I did not see you," says
the dragon.
"We were all hiding," say
the bees.

83

"Can I sing a song for you?" says the dragon.
"No! No! Please do not sing," they say.
The dragon looks sad.
"Nobody will let me sing," he says.
The dragon begins to cry.
They have never seen a dragon cry.

"Are you a real dragon?"
they say.
The dragon shows them
that he is.
He puffs smoke.
He spits fire.
They are all afraid.
They all run away.
"Come back," says the
dragon. "I will not hurt
you. I just want to sing."

"We will help you," say the birds. "Listen to us."
The dragon listens to the birds.
The dragon opens his mouth. He tries to sing like the birds. He cannot. He puffs smoke. He spits fire.
"Stop!" say the birds.
"Stop!" say the bees.
"Stop!" say the animals.

The dragon is sad. He walks away.

"Come back!" say the animals.

"We will help you," say the bees.

"How?" say the birds. "Bees cannot sing."

"We can hum," say the bees.

"Humming is like singing." The bees begin to hum.

"Can I do that?" says the dragon.
"You can if you try," say the bees.
The dragon tries to hum. He can do it. He can hum just like the bees. "Hum hum hum," hums the dragon.
Nobody tells him to stop.
"Hum hum hum," says the dragon.

H-M-M-M-M-M-M-M-M-M-M-M

H-M-M-M-M-M-M-M

H-M-M-M-M-M-M-M-M-M-M

Dragon is humming a
song.
The bees are humming too.
The birds are singing.
The animals join in.
The rabbits tap their feet.
The flowers nod their
heads.
They are all happy.

HM-MM-MM-MM-MM

HM-MM-MM-MM-MM-MM

HM-MM-MM-MM-MM-MM

Say these words again

listen	spits
mouth	their
asleep	join
animals	nobody
hiding	singing
afraid	hurt
humming	flowers

What are they doing?

sleeping

sitting

puffing

tapping

nodding

LITTLE HAMSTER

Little Hamster is in his garden. He is busy. He is digging.
Red Fox stops at the gate.
Red Fox gives Little Hamster a letter.
"Who is it from?" says Little Hamster.

"Open it and see," says
Red Fox. Little Hamster
opens the letter.
"It is from Big Hamster,"
he says,
"He is coming to stay with
me."
"When is he coming?"
says Red Fox.
"He is coming on
Monday," says Little
Hamster.

Little Hamster meets his friends.
"Big Hamster is coming to stay," says Little Hamster.
"When is he coming?" says Bob Hedgehog.
"He is coming on Monday," says Little Hamster.
"How is he coming?" says Polly Pig.
"He is coming by train," says Little Hamster.

Little Hamster waits for Big Hamster. His friends wait with him. Along comes the train. It stops. Big Hamster gets off the train.

"Hallo!" says Big Hamster.
"Hallo, Big Hamster," says Little Hamster.

"I will take the bag," says Bob Hedgehog.

107

They go to Little Hamster's house. Big Hamster unpacks his bag. He has a straw hat. He puts it on. He has a stick. He picks it up. Little Hamster sits on the bed. His friends sit on the bed. Big Hamster sings a song.

"Big Hamster sings on the stage," says Little Hamster.

Big Hamster can dance. He does a tap dance. His feet go tap, tap, tap.
Big Hamster likes to dance.
They all like to see Big Hamster dance.

Big Hamster is on the train.
Big Hamster is going
home.
"Goodbye," says Big
Hamster,
"Goodbye," says Little
Hamster.
"Goodbye," says Bob
Hedgehog.
"Goodbye," says Polly Pig.
"Goodbye," says Cheepy
Chick.
The train puffs away. Big
Hamster has gone.

The friends go home. They sit in the garden.

"I wish Big Hamster was here," says Little Hamster.

"So do I," says Bob Hedgehog.

"So do I," says Polly Pig.

"So do I," says Cheepy Chick.

They all look sad. They all feel sad.

Little Hamster gets up.

Little Hamster puts on a hat. He picks up a stick. "I will sing to you," he says.
"I will sing like Big Hamster." Little Hamster sings. He rolls his hat. He throws his stick. His friends clap. They still look sad. They still feel sad. They still wish Big Hamster was there.

Little Hamster wants his friends to smile. He gets on the table.

"What are you doing?" says Cheepy Chick.

"I am going to dance," says Little Hamster. "I am going to dance like Big Hamster."

Little Hamster tries to dance. He drops his stick. He drops his hat. His feet get mixed up. He looks very funny.

119

They all laugh.
"You are funny," says Bob
Hedgehog.
"You are funny," says
Polly Pig.
"You are funny," says
Cheepy Chick.
Little Hamster is so funny.
They think he is so funny.
They fall over.
Little Hamster is happy. His
friends are happy again.

"Watch me," says Little Hamster. He stands on one leg. He turns round.
"Oh!" says Little Hamster. "I am falling!"
Polly Pig catches him. He is not hurt.
"It is fun to dance," says Little Hamster. "Come and dance with me."

They all find a hat. They all find a stick. They all dance. They dance on the grass. It is safe on the grass. They will not be hurt if they fall.

"I wish Big Hamster could see us," says Little Hamster.

"So do I," says Bob Hedgehog.

"So do I," says Polly Pig.

"So do I," says Cheepy Chick.

Say these words again

garden	train
digging	catches
Monday	funny
friends	smile
unpacks	laugh
dance	goodbye
throws	mixed

What can you see?

letter

stick

hat

table

bag

127

DRAGON'S HIDING PLACE

Dragon lives in the wood.
The bees are his friends.
He hums songs with them.
One day, Rabbit comes to
see them.

Rabbit looks sad.

"Oh dear," says Rabbit.

"What is it?" says Dragon.

"What is it?" say the bees.

"There are men in the wood," says Rabbit.

"What do they want?" say the bees.

"They want Dragon," says Rabbit.

Dragon goes with Rabbit.
The bees go with Rabbit.
They see the men.
They hide behind a tree.
They watch. They listen.
The men have a net.
"We will catch the
dragon," say the men. "We
will put the dragon in a
cage."

Dragon looks for a place to hide. He sees a hole in a tree.

Dragon gets into the hole.

"What are you doing in the tree?" says Badger.

"I am hiding," says Dragon.

"I can see you," says Badger.

"What can I do?" says Dragon.

"Men are coming. They want to put me in a cage," says Dragon.
"I will help you," says Badger.
Badger rolls logs in front of the hole.
Nobody can see the hole.
Nobody can see Dragon.
Badger goes on his way.

The men come. They have
a net. They have sticks.
"Where is that dragon?"
say the men.
Dragon keeps very still.
The men do not see him.
The men go away.

It is safe. Dragon can come out.
Where is Dragon hiding?
Nobody knows.
The animals look for Dragon.
Nobody can find him.

145

Dragon is still inside the
tree. He knows it is safe to
come out.
He cannot get out.
He cannot move the logs.
"I will shout," says
Dragon. "The animals will
hear me."

Dragon opens his mouth.
But he knows he must not
shout.
He is a dragon. Dragons
spit fire when they shout.
Fire will burn the tree.
"I know what to do," says
Dragon.

149

Dragon begins to hum.
He hums as loud as he
can.
"Hum   Hum   HUM   HUM."
Dragon's friends hear the
humming.
"Only Dragon can hum like
that," say the bees. "He
must be inside the tree."

HM-HM-MM-MMM-MMM-MM-MM-MMM

They try to move the logs.
They cannot.
Badger comes to the tree.
Badger wants to help
Dragon.
"There is nobody in that
tree," says Badger.
"Yes, there is," says
Rabbit. "Dragon is in the
tree. We can hear him
humming."

"Dragon is our friend," say
the bees. "It is safe for him
to come out now."
"Then I will help you,"
says Badger.
They roll the logs away
from the hole.
Dragon gets out.
"I am glad to see you all,"
says Dragon.
"And we are glad to see
you," say his friends.

Say these words again

watch	sticks
loud	nobody
catch	shout
cage	fire
their	Badger
buzz	afraid
only	knows

What are they doing?

hopping

running

hiding

falling

helping

157

HEDGEHOG'S TALKING TREE

Bob Hedgehog likes to talk. He has a lot to say. He talks about the flowers. He talks about the trees. He talks about the sky. He talks about things he has done. He is always talking. He goes on and on talking.

Bob Hedgehog finds a
stone. It has a hole in it.
He wants to talk about the
stone. He sees Little
Hamster.
Little Hamster is digging.
"I want to tell you about
my stone," says Bob
Hedgehog.
Little Hamster is busy. He
does not want to stop.
"Tell me later," says Little
Hamster.

Bob Hedgehog sees Polly
Pig.
Polly Pig is washing.
"I want to tell you about
my stone," says Bob
Hedgehog.
Polly Pig is busy. She does
not want to stop.
"Tell me later," says Polly
Pig.

Bob Hedgehog sees
Cheepy Chick.
Cheepy Chick is dusting.
"I want to tell you about
my stone," says Bob
Hedgehog.
Cheepy Chick is busy. She
does not want to stop.
"Tell me later," says
Cheepy Chick.

No one will listen. They are all too busy.
Bob Hedgehog sees a tree.
"I want to tell you about my stone," says Bob Hedgehog.
The tree is not busy. The tree does not say, "Tell me later."
So, Bob Hedgehog tells the tree about his stone.

"I will tell all the trees,"
says Bob Hedgehog.
His friends see him talking
to the trees.
"Shall we play a trick?"
says Little Hamster.
"Yes," says Polly Pig.

Little Hamster hides behind
a tree. Bob Hedgehog talks
to the tree.
"I want to tell you about
my stone," says Bob
Hedgehog.
"What do you want to tell
me?" says Little Hamster.
Bob Hedgehog thinks the
tree is talking.

Bob Hedgehog looks
around. He must tell
someone about the talking
tree. There is no one to
tell. He tells the next tree.
"That tree can talk," he
says.
Polly Pig is hiding behind
the tree. "So can I," says
Polly Pig.
Bob Hedgehog thinks that
the tree is talking.

"I must tell someone,"
says Bob Hedgehog.
He sees Cheepy Chick.
He runs to her.
"Come with me," he says.
Cheepy Chick is busy. She
is sweeping. She does not
want to stop.
"Come with me," says Bob
Hedgehog. Cheepy Chick
has to go.

"That tree can talk," says
Bob Hedgehog.
"Trees cannot talk," says
Cheepy Chick.
"Say something, tree,"
says Bob Hedgehog.
The tree says nothing.
"I am going home," says
Cheepy Chick.
"Wait," says Bob
Hedgehog.

Bob Hedgehog takes
Cheepy Chick to the next
tree.
"That tree can talk," he
says. "Say something,
tree."
The tree says nothing.
"Are you playing a trick on
me?" asks Cheepy Chick.
"No," says Bob Hedgehog.
He shakes his head. "It
must have been a dream,"
he says.

Little Hamster is hiding
behind the tree.
"It was not a dream," says
Little Hamster.
Bob Hedgehog thinks it is
the tree talking.
"I told you trees can talk,"
says Bob Hedgehog.
Cheepy Chick knows trees
cannot talk. She goes
behind the tree. She sees
Little Hamster.

"It was Little Hamster talking," says Cheepy Chick.
"I was playing a trick on you," says Little Hamster.
Polly Pig comes out. "So was I," she says.
Bob Hedgehog says nothing.
He just does not know what to say.

Say these words again

things   listen

talking   always

dream   does

stone   nothing

busy   thinks

trick   shakes

behind   know

What are they doing?

digging

washing

hiding

dusting

sweeping

187

Here is Dragon again.
What is Dragon doing?
Dragon tells the rabbits
a story. The rabbits
listen. Dragon knows
lots of stories.

Can you make up a story?
Say these words again

rabbits	story
listen	knows

What are they doing?

hopping

crying

peeping

hiding

listening

189